Thursday	Friday	Saturday	Sunday

ONLY YOU

ROSEMARY WELLS

VIKING

VIKING
Published by the Penguin Group
Penguin Putnam Books for Young Readers,
345 Hudson Street, New York, New York 10014, U.S.A.

Penguin Books Ltd, Registered Offices: Harmondsworth, Middlesex, England

First published in 2003 by Viking,
a division of Penguin Putnam Books for Young Readers.

1   3   5   7   9   10   8   6   4   2

LIBRARY OF CONGRESS CATALOGING-IN-PUBLICATION DATA:
Wells, Rosemary.
Only you / by Rosemary Wells.
p. cm.
Summary: A little bear describes how much his mother means to him.
ISBN 0-670-03634-X
[1. Mother and child—Fiction. 2. Bears—Fiction.] I. Title.
PZ7.W46843 On 2003
[E]—dc21
2002015570

Manufactured in China
Set in Minister

ONLY YOU

For Rachel Hodges

Only you can show me I can do
anything I try!

I'm the apple of your eye.
Only you.

Only you . . .
don't mind what I do.

Over goes your coffee cup,
but you laugh and pick it up.
Only you.

Only you . . .
can make my dreams come true.

Dreams lie sleeping in my heart,
waiting for my world to start.
Only you.

Only you . . .
can turn my gray sky blue.
Without you near,

I feel so very small.
How I wait to hear
your footsteps in the hall.

The only place I want to be
is in your lap or on your knee.

Only you.
Only me.

The first three years of a child's life are important in so many ways. Young children learn by living. Everything they see and do helps them understand the world and how it works. When parents spend time with their children, the children grow and glory in the special attention of the people they know and love best. In the games and rituals that develop around household chores, errands, mealtime, naps, playtime, and bedtime, children find security, comfort, and the courage to explore. From close relationships with their parents, young children learn what it is to be loved.

Children make remarkable developmental progress in the first three years of life—learning language, social skills, and physical coordination. They learn to play with other people and to understand that other people have needs and feelings. It's a joy to watch your child grow and develop. Parents can encourage this development—not by "teaching" their children lessons, not by buying them lavish educational equipment, but by giving them one-on-one time. This positive parental attention shows children, over and over, that they are loved. With this knowledge, children will build the basic security and confidence that they need to take on the world.

—*Dr. Perri Klass*

FILL EVERY DAY OF YOUR CHILD'S YEAR

	Monday	Tuesday	Wednesday
praising	★	★	★
holding	★	★	★
reading stories	★	★	★
playing games	★	★	★
singing songs	★	★	★
talking	★	★	★
eating together	★	★	★
listening	★	★	★
kisses & hugs	★	★	★